BUSY DAYS WITH
Curious George®

Curious George Goes to the Zoo © 2011 by Houghton Mifflin Harcourt Publishing Company
Curious George and the Ice Cream Surprise © 2011 by Houghton Mifflin Harcourt Publishing Company
Curious George Saves His Pennies © 2012 by Houghton Mifflin Harcourt Publishing Company
Curious George Visits the Dentist © 2014 by Houghton Mifflin Harcourt Publishing Company
Curious George Goes to a Bookstore © 2014 by Houghton Mifflin Harcourt Publishing Company
Curious George Joins the Team © 2015 by Houghton Mifflin Harcourt Publishing Company
Curious George Says Thank You © 2011 by Houghton Mifflin Harcourt Publishing Company
Curious George and the Sleepover © 2016 by Houghton Mifflin Harcourt Publishing Company

Based on the character of Curious George®, created by Margret and H. A. Rey.
Curious George® is a registered trademark of Houghton Mifflin Harcourt Publishing Company.

ISBN: 978-1-328-69598-7

Manufactured in China
SCP 10 9 8 7 6 5 4 3 2 1

4500659635

BUSY DAYS WITH

Curious George®

8 STORIES INCLUDED

MARGRET AND H. A. REY

HOUGHTON MIFFLIN HARCOURT
BOSTON NEW YORK

Contents

MARGRET & H.A. REY'S
Curious George
Goes to the Zoo

Written by Cynthia Platt

Illustrated in the style of H. A. Rey by Mary O'Keefe Young

This is George. George is a good little monkey and always
very curious. Today, George was feeling very excited.
The man with the yellow hat was taking him to the zoo!

As they drove, the man explained to George that this wasn't just any
zoo that they were going to visit.

"It's called the Wild Animal Park," the man said. "All of the animals roam around freely."

When they arrived, George saw a huge banner. George looked up at it, but he could not read the words.

COME CELEBRATE OUR BABY RHINO'S 1st BIRTHDAY PARTY

ZOO

A friendly zookeeper explained.

"It's an extra-special day here at the Wild Animal Park," she said. "It is our baby rhino's first birthday. We are going to have a party for her later on!"

A party! This was going to be a wonderful trip to the zoo.

George tried to walk into the park where the animals were, but the zookeeper stopped him.

"You can't walk in there!" she said.

"To explore this zoo, you have ride in one of our special cars."
She pointed to a huge car that had no roof on it.

Oh, my! What fun this was going to be.
   George and his friend climbed onboard and the
car drove into the park.

Soon they were in the midst of the Wild Animal Park.

"Look over there!" said the zookeeper. "There's our pride of lions. We have a large family here."

10

George pointed in the other direction. "Yes, George," said the zookeeper. "I see the giraffes, too. Their tall necks help them eat leaves from the tree-tops. And there are two ostriches running this way!"

George was happy to be seeing so many amazing animals.

11

The zoo car drove past a small pond. Pink flamingos waded in the water. Their heads bobbed up and down as they walked on spindly legs.

"The flamingos turn pink because they eat so many tiny pink shrimp," said the zoo-keeper, but George was not listening.

He had never seen flamingos before. He was curious about how those flamingos were moving.

He leaned out the back of the zoo car as far as he could to take a look. But then—oh! What happened?!

First George lost his balance. Then he fell—*kerplunk!*—right out of the zoo car. His friend hadn't noticed that he had fallen. George ran as quickly as a little monkey could toward the pond.

The flamingos bobbed their heads and lifted their feet one at a time. It looked like they were dancing. George danced with them.

Suddenly, the water in the pond started to move. Then a hippo popped its head out from under the water. What a surprise! George stopped dancing to take a look.

The hippo opened its huge mouth as if it were yawning. George opened his mouth wide, too. It was fun to act like the hippo!

Just then, George noticed that something was rustling in the reeds near the pond. George was curious. He wanted to see what was there.

In an instant, he jumped over to the reeds. He poked his nose inside and saw . . . a baby rhino!

The tiny rhino was cute, but she looked a little bit sad and a little bit lonely.

George wanted to make that
baby rhino feel happy again.
He thought and thought.
Maybe the baby rhino would
like the flamingo dance.

He jumped and bobbed
his head and danced his
feet up and down.

The baby rhino peeked her head out of the reeds so that she could watch. George danced more, and the rhino walked out of the reeds.

She was curious, too!

They were having so much fun that George didn't notice what was behind him.

The zookeeper stomped over to George. She did not look happy. The man with the yellow hat was running behind her.

"You are a naughty little monkey," said the zookeeper. "You were supposed to stay in the car. You and your friend will have to go now."

George walked to the man's side. He waved goodbye to the baby rhino. The man and the zookeeper turned to see whom George was waving to.

"The baby rhino! Why, we've been looking for her all day," said the zookeeper. "She got separated from her mother."

George was glad to see the zookeeper looking happy again. He and the man started walking toward the exit.

The zookeeper ran to stop them. "Thank you for finding our baby rhino, George. And just in time for her birthday party. Will you join us for some cake?"

George jumped with glee. He had forgotten about the party, and he did love cake.

The man and George followed the zookeeper and the baby
rhino back to zoo headquarters. The rhino's mother was
waiting there for her.

The zookeeper brought out a special birthday cake that was shaped like a rhino. George had never seen a cake like that before.

"You can have the first piece, George," said the zookeeper. "I also have a special treat, just for you!" She placed a bunch of bananas in front of him.

George was very happy to have a tasty banana, but he saved room for some cake, too!

MARGRET & H.A. REY'S
Curious George
and the Ice Cream Surprise

Written by Monica Perez

Illustrated in the style of H. A. Rey by Mary O'Keefe Young

George was a good little monkey and always very curious.

One hot afternoon he heard, *Jingle-jingle. Jingle-jingle.*
What could that music be? George was curious about
the melody he heard coming in through the window.

"That's an ice cream truck, George," said the man with the yellow hat. "You know summertime is here when you start hearing the music of the ice cream truck."

George loved trucks, and he loved ice cream. Ice cream would taste
so good on a hot day like today! He would find this wonderful ice
cream truck right away. He started to climb out the window, but
his friend stopped him. George had to finish his lunch first.

By the time George rushed out the door, the music was gone.

"Don't worry, George," the man said. "The ice cream truck makes a trip around town each day, all summer long. We'll catch the ice cream truck tomorrow."

The next day it got hotter and hotter. George waited for the ice cream truck, but there was no sight or sound of it.

"Let's go to the pool, George," said the man with the yellow hat. George ran to get his towel. Splashing around in the pool would be a great way to beat the heat!

But the pool was closed for renovation.

"Look on the bright side, George. By autumn, we'll have a larger pool with three diving boards. Won't that be fun?"

It did sound fun. But George needed to cool off now, not in the autumn!

So, George went back to waiting for the ice cream truck.
He dreamed of vanilla, chocolate, and strawberry ice
cream bars.

George thought he heard the
music of the ice cream truck once . . .

. . . but it was just a little boy's harmonica.

George and his neighbors decided to go to the park to run through the sprinklers. But just as they arrived, the sprinklers were turned off.

It was a long walk back home. Luckily for George, there was lemonade waiting for him on the porch.

George took a drink and made a face. It was warm.

"Sorry, George," the man with the yellow hat said.
"Our freezer has decided to stop working. All our
ice cubes have melted."

Now would be the perfect time to hear the sweet sound of
the ice cream truck. Wait—was that it? Yes, there was the
truck turning the corner now!

"Wave it down, George. I'll be right back with my wallet!"
The man rushed back into the house.

But the ice cream truck driver could not see the little
monkey on the curb. The truck was not driving very
quickly, but it was driving away!

George looked back at his house.
He looked at the truck.

Then he had an idea.

George climbed a tree

and swung
from branch

to branch

until he swung right onto
the roof of the truck.

He rode the truck into town.
The truck stopped beside the
town park.

ICE CREAM

A window on the side opened up, and a small child and her mother stopped to buy ice cream.

George could not believe his eyes. The little girl had ordered a frozen treat that looked exactly like a chocolate-covered banana! George danced happily. He knew exactly what to order. The little girl saw him and laughed.

So many people wanted ice cream that
the driver ran out of change. He hurried
over to the nearby bank to get more.

Meanwhile, George noticed that the ice cream line was getting
very long. Everyone looked hot. There was no shade to stand in.
Maybe he could help.

George jumped down into the truck, where it was dark and cool.
He grabbed as many ice cream bars, cones, and ice pops as he could.
He handed them out to the waiting children, their parents . . .
and even their pets!

George worked so quickly, he didn't remember to collect money for the ice cream. No one seemed to mind—except the ice cream man!

"What have you done?" he cried when he returned. "Half my ice cream is gone!" George climbed up a telephone pole. George was very glad to see his friend hurrying toward the park.

"Hold on a minute," said a voice below. "Look at how everyone is enjoying themselves! It's been the hottest summer in town history. An ice cream social is exactly what we need."

It was the mayor, and she offered to pay for everyone's ice cream. "Thank you, George, for your great idea. I think the town should sponsor an ice cream party every summer!"

The ice cream truck driver was happy to keep
serving ice cream. George and the man with the
yellow hat helped.

The ice cream man saved one last treat for George—
a chocolate-covered banana-cicle! Delicious!

MARGRET & H.A. REY'S

Curious George
Visits the Dentist

Written by Monica Perez

illustrated in the style of H. A. Rey by Mary O'Keefe Young

George was a good little monkey and always very curious.

When he visited his neighbor Mrs. Ross, he was especially curious about her gleaming basket of fruit. That bright red apple on top looked too perfect to be true.

And it was! George bit into it and discovered that it was hard and sticky and not sweet.

"Oh, dear," said Mrs. Ross. "That's not a real apple, George. It's made of wax."

George's tooth began to hurt. "You should always ask before eating something, George," the man with the yellow hat reminded him.

By the time he went to bed that evening, George's tooth was less sore. But the next morning his tooth was wobbly!

His mouth felt so strange that George couldn't even enjoy his favorite pancake breakfast.

"We should see the dentist, George," the man said. "She can make sure that tooth of yours is all right."

The man explained that the dentist was a doctor for teeth, but George didn't want anyone to touch his tooth. What if it hurt?

George walked along the path to the dentist's office with his friend, his steps getting slower and slower until . . . he ran off to pick a daisy.

"That's very pretty," said the man, chasing after George.
"But we have an appointment and we shouldn't be late.
You'll be a good little monkey, won't you?"

George nodded. He always wanted to be good.

The waiting room was a welcoming place.

There were lots of things to see and do. One by one, the young patients were called away by a woman in a white suit. George watched them go through a red door, each holding on to a grownup's hand.

One frightened boy was carried in by his mother. George was glad he wouldn't have to see the dentist by himself.

"George, you're next," the woman announced. George was sad to put down his book, but he was also a little curious about where the children were going.

Was there a play area on the other side?

The examining room was not filled with toys, but it was still interesting.

There was a sink and a long chair for lying down. There was a stool for the dentist and a light above the chair.

George was curious. Why were there two faucets in the room?

"Hello, George. I'm Dr. Wang. It's nice to meet you," she said. "Why don't you lie down and we'll take a look at your teeth?"

George saw a row of silver dental exam tools on the counter. They were long, shiny, and pointy. He hid behind the man.

"George, would you like me to try out the chair first?" the man asked.

"Great idea!" said Dr. Wang.

The man lay down.
"Open your mouth wide." The dentist shined the big light down into the man's mouth. She took out a small white instrument to take a closer look at each tooth. "This is a mouth mirror."

George watched. It didn't look too scary.

"Next I'll count the teeth," Dr. Wang told George.

She picked up one of those sharp, pointy tools. "This is an explorer. One, two, three, four . . ."

Then the man exclaimed, "Ow!"

"Uh-oh," the dentist said.

George ran away.

He left the exam room and scurried down the hall.
There were many doors. He didn't know which was the way out.

He tried one door and walked into another exam room.

"A monkey!" a little girl cried, and jumped off the exam
chair in excitement as George backed out of the room.

He continued down the hall, opening doors and disturbing patients. In
one room the scared little boy from
the reception area was crying.

George had an idea.
He jumped onto a table and began
juggling packs of dental floss. The
little boy stopped crying and smiled.

Next George leaped over to the sink in the middle of the
room. He pushed a button and the nearby water jet spurted,
spraying water around the room.

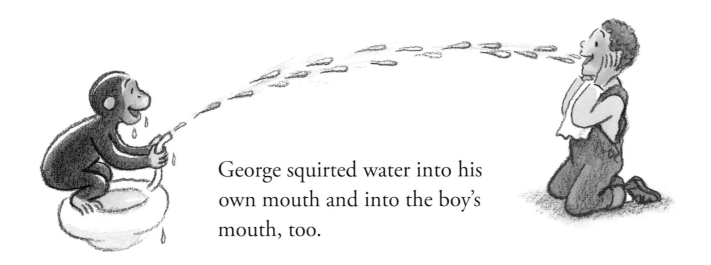

George squirted water into his own mouth and into the boy's mouth, too.

Next, George decided to switch on the overhead lamp, but the lamp tumbled over, spilling George safely on the floor.

The boy clapped.

But . . . uh-oh. Dr. Wang stood in the doorway.

"George, you naughty monkey!" Dr. Wang said. "What a mess you've made."

"This monkey was the
only one who could get
Tyler to stop crying,"
the boy's mother said.

"Hmm." Dr. Wang considered. She said, "It does look like we have some eager young patients. And if it weren't for you, George, I wouldn't have found the cavity in your friend's mouth."

"Turns out I need to have a filling," the man with the yellow hat said. "Come on, George, let's both get our teeth checked!"

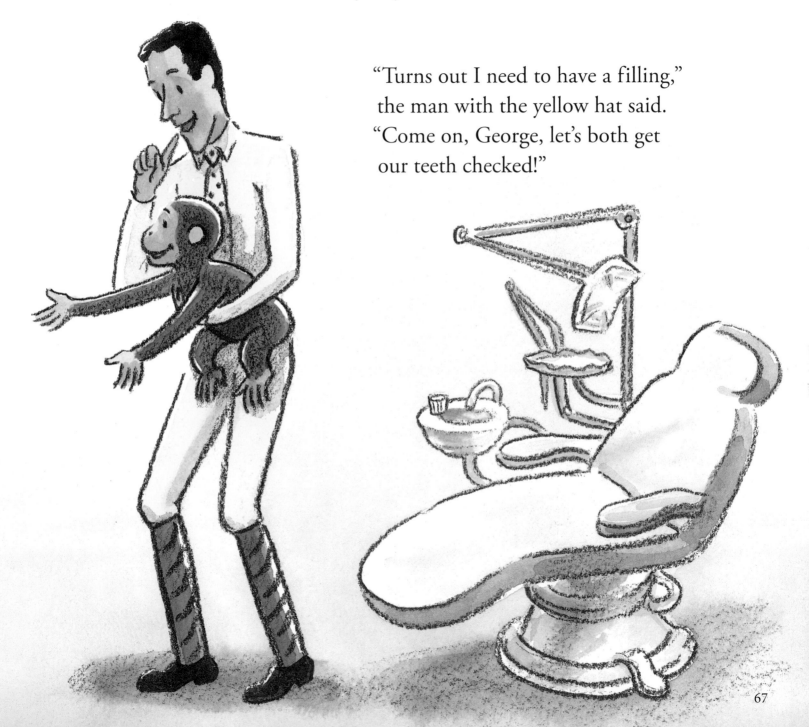

As soon as Dr. Wang looked into George's mouth, she laughed. "Why, George, all you have is a loose tooth!" A loose tooth sounded worrisome to George. "It's going to fall out soon. There's a new, permanent tooth right behind it. Looks like you've been doing a good job brushing your teeth."

George jumped on his chair. He did. He brushed every night and morning.

"Keep brushing and don't eat too many sweets," the dentist reminded him.
"You want your teeth to be in good shape for the tooth fairy."

George waved goodbye to his new friends. He went home with a new toothbrush, some dental floss, and instructions for his loose tooth—he should bite into as many hard apples as he could, as long as they were real, of course.

He decided he didn't mind going to the dentist at all. That night he ate a healthy dinner with an apple for dessert. His tooth fell out with his second bite.

He put his tooth under his pillow.

When Mrs. Ross came to check on George that afternoon,
George proudly showed her his coin from the tooth fairy.
Mrs. Ross laughed and said, "Well, that was a quick way to
lose a tooth. But I don't recommend it next time!"

MARGRET & H.A. REY'S

Curious George
Saves His Pennies

Written by Monica Perez

Illustrated by Mary O'Keefe Young

George was a good little monkey and always very curious, especially when he was in Tammy's Toy Store.

There were so many things to wonder about . . .
pogo sticks and skateboards,

snow globes
and kaleidoscopes,

and even finger traps.

But George's favorite thing to do in the
toy store was play at the train table.
Today there was a new train.
Its wood was painted bright
red, and it had a real
working whistle.

George held it up to show his friend, the man with the yellow hat.
"Not today," his friend said.

"We're looking for a
birthday present for Noah,
remember? He's turning five.
What do you think of this?"

George helped his friend pick out
a yellow and green hula hoop.
While Tammy the shopkeeper
wrapped the present for the
birthday party, George
wandered back to
the train table.

"I have a suggestion, George," said the man as he carried the gift over.

"Why don't you buy that new train yourself? The tag says $5.00. I'm sure you can save the money for it."

George liked this suggestion so much that he was only a little sorry to put the train back down.

George had a good time at the birthday party. Noah let everyone have a turn at the hula hoop. It was harder than it looked!

As soon as George got home that afternoon, he took his piggy bank down from his dresser. He opened the small plug at the bottom and shook. Out tumbled a nickel. George ran to show the coin to his friend.

"You have five cents," the man said. "I'll give you your allowance early this week. Don't spend it on candy. You have to save it up." The man gave George two quarters.

"Here is fifty cents," he said. "Now you have fifty-five cents. You have only $4.45 left to save."

George wasn't quite sure how much money that was, but it sounded like a lot.

George dreamed about his red train that night. He was riding it through a forest of trees. He tugged on the whistle again and again so that no one could miss such a shiny red engine!

In the morning, George decided he would have to find a way to earn money faster. What if someone else were to buy the red train at the toy store before he could?

He had an idea.

He found a nickel under his bed.

His piggy bank jingled nicely that evening. He had seventy-five cents saved. One more quarter and he would have a dollar!

The next morning George had another idea. He would get a job.

Lucky for George, his neighbor Mr. Reddy needed help raking leaves. George worked all morning long, gathering armfuls of red, brown, and gold leaves to add to a growing pile in the center of the yard. Mr. Reddy brought out lemonade for the two to share. While his neighbor rested on the sun porch swing, George climbed a tree.

The pile of leaves looked tempting from above.
George wondered what would happen if . . .

Before he finished wondering, he had swung out of the branches and right
into the center of the pile. The leaves crunched and crumbled and swooshed
and swirled. What an adventure!

What hard work it was raking the
leaves back up!

But at the end of the day, Mr. Reddy paid
him two dollars. George had $2.75 saved.
That was almost three dollars.

George spent many days doing odd jobs.

He washed windows.

He distributed flyers.

He delivered flowers.

He did dishes.

At the end of a week, George
finally had $5.00.

    "I'm proud of you, George,"
said the man with the
yellow hat.

    "You saved all that money
by yourself. You've sure earned
that train."

    The change clinked merrily in the piggy bank as George
set off for the toy store. The autumn day was bright and clear
and not very cold. George walked by the park.

The neighborhood children were playing with a windsock. Suddenly, it got stuck in a tree. They needed George's help!

George carefully set his piggy bank down on a nearby park bench where he could keep an eye on it. But little monkeys sometimes forget. And as George began to play with the children, he forgot to check that his bank was still there.

89

As the afternoon wore on, his friends went home to have dinner. George rushed to the park bench where he had left his piggy bank. The toy store might be closing soon. But his bank was gone!

Maybe George had the wrong bench?

There were many in
the park, after all.

But he was disappointed each time
he ran up to another empty bench.

George walked home sadly. He wondered how long it would take him to
save five dollars again. As George passed the toy store, he happened to look
through the window. He couldn't believe his eyes. A little girl was holding
his piggy bank!

George rushed into the toy store just as the girl's mother was saying, "We found this across the street and waited for its owner, but it's getting late. We saw it has the name of your store on the bottom. Can you keep it in case someone comes to claim it?"

George jumped up and down on the counter. "Why, George!" Tammy said. "Is the piggy bank yours? You're lucky Hana and her mother found it."

Hugging his piggy bank tightly, George rushed over to the train section. He located the shiny red engine right away.

As he carried it to the counter, the little girl looked at his train shyly.

George realized he had not said thank you to her for keeping
his savings safe. He looked at his train. He looked at his piggy bank. He
looked at Hana. Good deeds deserve to be rewarded, he decided. George
set the train down. He upended his bank on
the counter and began to sort
dollars and coins.

George and Hana walked out of the toy store that day each carrying a train. George's small engine was not red, but it was shiny and blue and he had paid for it all by himself. Best of all, he had a new friend who loved to play with trains almost as much as he did.

MARGRET & H.A. REY'S
Curious George
Goes to a Bookstore

Written by Julie M. Bartynski

Illustrated in the style of H. A. Rey by Mary O'Keefe Young

Georg was a good little monkey and always very curious.

Today George and his friend the man with the yellow hat were going to the grand opening of a bookstore in their neighborhood. George's favorite author was going to be signing her latest Penny the Penguin picture book. He had every Penny book she'd ever written. He couldn't wait to meet her.

But when they arrived at the bookstore, they found a long line that zigzagged between the bookshelves. "We'll purchase the book first and then wait in line to get it signed," said his friend. "There are a lot of kids who also love Penny the Penguin!"

The line inched forward and stopped, inched forward and stopped.
George climbed onto his friend's shoulders and tried to take a peek at
the author, but he was small and she was hidden by the crowd.

He looked around the bookstore. So many new books! What stories would they hold inside? What funny characters would he meet?

"Be a good little monkey and don't wander off too far," said the man with the yellow hat, letting George down and picking up a bird-watching guide from a nearby shelf. "You wouldn't want to miss getting your book signed."

George was happily flipping through storybooks when he noticed the wonderful smell of banana bread. It made his stomach rumble. George was curious. Could there be food in a bookstore? Food and drink were never allowed in the library. George decided to find out.

As soon as he turned the corner, he discovered glass shelves filled with baked goods instead of books! It was a small café.

Next to the cabinet was a table with a sign advertising free samples.

George watched people help themselves to little squares of banana bread. He took one too. Yum!

A little girl saw George and tugged on her father's sleeve.
"Daddy, look! That monkey likes banana bread too!"

"Yes, I suppose monkeys would
enjoy banana bread," he responded,
still looking at his book.

While George was reaching for another sample, and then another and another, he saw the little girl and her father leave the café area. Tucked under the girl's arm was George's favorite dinosaur book.

He decided to follow them.

They led him past a display of dinosaur books in the science area of the store. The display was as tall as the man with the yellow hat. It was hard to resist for a little monkey who loves to climb!

George climbed onto the first tier. With so many books to look at, he wasn't sure where to start! He saw his favorite dinosaur book, but he also saw other books. One pictured an apatosaurus eating leaves and another showed pterodactyls soaring above waterfalls.

He climbed from tier to tier until he reached the top. From above he noticed a stack of boxes in the corner of the store. The boxes were shaped like presents, but the bows and wrapping paper were missing.

What could be inside them?

George leaped down
and opened the boxes.

They each contained
a stack of the newest
Penny the Penguin
picture book!

George wondered: Why were the books in boxes? They should be in a big display like the dinosaur books.

George had an idea.

George got to work right away.
He balanced the books one by one,
as if he were building with blocks.

People in line marveled at what he
was doing—except for the man with
the yellow hat, who was engrossed in
his new bird-watching guide.

The tower of books grew
and grew and grew, and so did
the crowd's amazement.

"What a wonderful display,"
said a woman.

"Wow, look what that monkey
made!" exclaimed a little boy.

"Stop!" shouted a nearby bookseller.
"You shouldn't have opened those boxes!"

But George
was having too
much fun to
notice.

From the top of his display, George looked down and finally saw the bookseller, the manager, and the man with the yellow hat peering up at him.

"That monkey opened all our boxes for the signing," complained the bookseller.

The manager smiled at George. "He certainly did, and now we don't have to. I think his tower of books is a masterpiece!"

The manager asked George if he would like to help with the signing. George was delighted. He would finally get to meet his favorite author!

George made sure each book was opened to the right page, ready for the author's signature. He thought it was funny that her name was Penny, just like the penguin in her books.

As she finished signing the last book, Penny turned to George and smiled. "Thank you so much for all of your help today. It was great to have the extra hands and feet! But there's one book I still need to sign."

She inscribed the book and handed it to George. Inside was
a note saying, "To my new friend George. Keep reading!"

George loved his new book. It was special and one of a kind. He'd had such an adventurous day at the bookstore, he couldn't wait to visit again.

MARGRET & H.A.REY'S
Curious George
Joins the Team

Written by Cynthia Platt

Illustrated in the style of H. A. Rey by Mary O'Keefe Young

This is George.
George is a good little monkey
and always very curious.

NEW PLAYGROUND FOR ALL KIDS

This morning, George had a playdate at a brand-new playground. George
loves playgrounds. And anything new is always exciting!

George was going to meet his new friend, Tina, at the playground. "You're going to love this park, George," the man with the yellow hat told him.

"There's a basketball court and a special play structure that was built so that children with or without disabilities can all play together."

George tried to imagine what this special playground might look like as they drove there.

When George and his friend
pulled into the playground, the
park looked even better than he
had dreamed!

There was a giant castle in the middle with wide ramps
to run up and down. There were special swings—some
that had great comfy seats, and one that could fit a
wheelchair. George saw Tina on a swing!

As the man with the yellow hat talked to Tina's grandmother, George studied the play structure. Could he do everything in this new playground in just one day? He thought so . . .

He ran up a ramp just as Tina sped up behind him. George loved the way Tina raced around the play structure on four wheels. She was amazing!

First he climbed the monkey bars.
He was very good at this!

Then Tina zoomed down
a cool wide slide. She was
very good at that.

Next, they played tic-tac-toe. They were both very good at tic-tac-toe!

The sound of a ball bouncing distracted George.
There was a group of kids throwing an orange
ball into a hoop. George and Tina raced over to
watch them.

Tina was very excited.

"I love to play basketball!" she said.
Her grandmother came over.

"Why don't you ask if you can
join?" she said. But Tina was too shy
to ask, and she looked a little sad.

George tried to cheer her up. He jumped as high as he could
and swung all around the trees over her head. Tina laughed as
she watched him. The kids on the basketball court stopped to
watch too.

"I'm Jenna. And we're the Slam Dunkers," a girl told George. "Do you want to come and play with our team?"

He had never played basketball before. He was so curious, he forgot he was playing with Tina. He ran off onto the court and took the ball.

Basketball was so much fun!
George learned to dribble
the ball and throw it to his
teammates.

He was super at jump-
ing up to catch the ball
when it rebounded off
the backboard.

During a break Tina wheeled her chair onto the basketball court.
"Can I play too?" she asked in a quiet voice. George hoped
they'd be on the same team!

But the other kids weren't so sure.

"You play basketball?" Jenna asked.

"Sure, I play all the time," answered Tina.

Then George had an idea. He got the ball, and with one quick leap, he threw it to Tina!

Tina looked surprised, but
then she wheeled onto the
court. She shot—and she
scored!

Tina was a great basketball player!

"Like I said, I play a lot at home," she reminded them.

"I can tell," said Jenna. "We play every week. Do you and George want to join our team?"

George and Tina played basketball all afternoon. They even made plans to come and play together another day soon. Tina and George were part of the team now, and they always scored the most baskets!

MARGRET & H.A.REY'S
Curious George
Says Thank You

Written by Emily Flaschner Meyer and Julie M. Bartynski

Illustrated in the style of H. A. Rey by Anna Grossnickle Hines

This is George.
He was a good little monkey and always very curious.
Today George received a surprise in the mail. "It looks like
you got a card, George," said the man with the yellow hat.

It was a thank-you card from George's neighbor Betsy.

Dear George,
Thank you so much for the birthday present. I'm putting the stickers you gave me on every-thing. Even this card!
Sincerely,
Betsy

The card made George smile. It also made him curious.
Who could he give a thank-you card to? George thought
and thought.

He could send one to the science museum director, Dr. Lee, who had shown George her favorite collection of dinosaur fossils. Of course, there was also the librarian who helped him pick out books. Hmm . . . The store clerk at the market always saved the best bananas for him. And his friend Bill let George fly his kite in the park.

George had so many people to thank—he had to get started
right away!
First he gathered paper, envelopes, crayons, and stickers.
Then he got to work.

The man with the yellow hat walked in to find George
covered from head to toe.
"Uh-oh, George! What are you doing?"

George held up Betsy's card and pointed to the papers scattered around him.

"Oh, I see, George," said his friend. "You're making your own thank-you cards. What a nice idea. Would you like some help?"

The man wrote while George decorated. George was having so much fun that they even made a stack of extra cards. "We can hand-deliver these tomorrow. Everyone will be happy to see you, George."

Their first stop was the science museum.
"George, it's so good to see you," said Dr. Lee. "What a lovely card! I'm going to hang it in my office right now."

Next they stopped at the library. "What a great card," the librarian said. "I'm going to set it here on my desk where everyone can see it. George, we have some new books in the children's section that you might like, if you have time." George looked at his friend. "All right," the man said. "I will go get a book for myself."

George noticed the mail carrier leaving the library. She was the one who had brought George his thank-you card in the first place. He wanted to give her one of his cards too! George hurried out the door. Could he catch her in time?

George jumped up and down on the steps, waving a card, but a group of children was just getting off a bus. They were coming to the library for story hour. George couldn't see which way the mail carrier had gone.

But, oh! There was a streetlight nearby. George was curious.
Maybe if he climbed it, he could see where the mail carrier
was going.

George started to climb the streetlight as fast as only a monkey can. But when he was halfway up the pole, his bag slipped off.

In an instant, all of George's thank-you cards went whirling through the air.
Oh, no! How would George deliver his cards now?

George slid down the pole and grabbed at the cards swirling around him.

A boy looked up. "Hey! It's snowing mail!"

A little girl said, "Don't worry, little monkey. We'll help you pick up your cards."

The children gathered up the cards. George was very grateful
for their help. He was also grateful that he had brought extra
cards. He decided to give them to all of the children.
"These cards are so nice!" said the teacher.

The man with the yellow hat came hurrying down the steps. "George! I didn't see you leave. It looks like you've had quite an adventure out here."
The man thanked the teacher and his students for helping George.

"Let's finish delivering those thank-you cards," said the man.
George and his friend stopped by the market and the park
and then headed home.

George felt a little sad that he hadn't caught up to the mail carrier. But wait! Who was that at George's house?

George proudly gave her a thank-you card.
"Wow, George!" said the mail carrier. "I'm usually
the one delivering the cards. This sure is a treat!"

George waved goodbye, and he and the man went into their house.

But George had one more very special thank-you card to deliver.

He had saved the best for last!

MARGRET & H.A.REY'S
Curious George
and the Sleepover

Written by Monica Perez

Illustrated in the style of H. A. Rey by Anna Grossnickle Hines

George is a good little monkey and always very curious.

George's curiosity helped him make friends everywhere. Tallulah and Jarrod were his good friends from down the street. They lived with their dad and Gramma Willa.

On weekends they
liked to spend time
together. Gramma Willa took
them swimming,
to the zoo, or to the park.

One day, Jarrod had some news.
"My dad is leaving this weekend for
a work trip. Gramma is planning a
special fun night on Saturday! We
get to watch a movie, eat popcorn with
real butter, and go to bed half
an hour late."

Tallulah added, "Gramma says you can spend the night
with us, and in the morning we can make waffles!"

A sleepover sounded wonderful to George. The man with the yellow hat agreed to the plan. Hooray!

It was only Wednesday, so George had plenty of time to prepare for his first sleepover. He was curious about his new sleeping bag, so he tried it out.

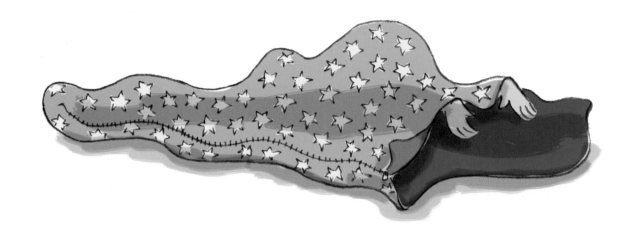

On Thursday he borrowed the man's backpack. He would need his toothbrush, his pajamas, his alarm clock with the bird that chirped on top, a flashlight . . . and snacks!

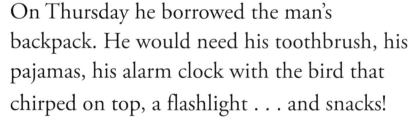

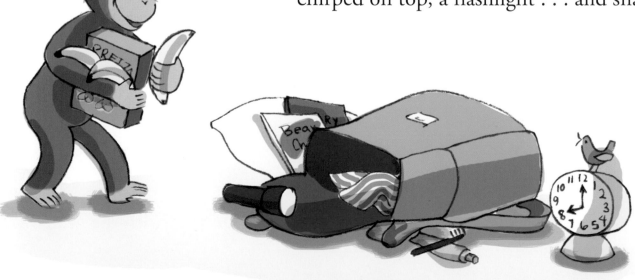

On Friday, George had to pack more snacks because he had eaten all the banan-as in the bag.

Then he packed two suitcases full of toys. His friend suggested that George might want to travel with less . . . so George settled on taking his favorite toy, Lola.

On Saturday, George was still excited, but a funny feeling had begun to settle in the pit of his stomach . . . It started out small, as if maybe George had eaten too many cookies. But as the day wore on, the feeling began to grow.

The doorbell rang. Tallulah and Jarrod burst through the door, chattering away about their plans for the evening. They had made George a red sash with blue letters that said "Guest of Honor"!

For a moment, George forgot about being worried.
He proudly wore the sash down the street and into his
friends' house. Even when it came time for George to say
goodbye to the man with the yellow hat, George didn't
remember he had been nervous, because he was helping
Tallulah set up a tent in the living room.

George and his friends had a
busy evening.
They watched a movie
and ate popcorn.

They had a pillow fight.

When it was time for
bed, they brushed their
teeth, changed into
PJs, and climbed into
the tent. Tallulah and
Jarrod fell right
to sleep.

179

But George didn't. The floor was a little hard.
He missed his bed at home. He stared at the shadows on the
ceiling of the tent. Was that a bear?

George's stomach did a little flip. He peeked out the tent flap and saw that it was only the coat rack casting shadows on the tent. He settled back onto his pillow. But then he heard a soft scratching sound.

He jumped out of the tent with Lola safely in hand. He looked out the window and saw the branches of an apple tree scratching the side of the house. How silly of him to worry!

George had an idea. He would make himself some warm milk. That always helped him sleep at home.

George poured himself a mug of milk. Oops. He would have to clean that spill up later. He wasn't quite sure how to go about warming up the milk. He knew not to touch the stove.

At home, his friend always heated the milk for him. So George just arranged some cookies on a plate. Yum—they would go nicely with the milk.

But holding on to a full mug and the cookies was hard work. He spilled more milk onto the floor.

George put down the cookies and went looking for a mop.
There it was. Oh, no! He accidentally swiped the mop across
the table. Cookies went flying!

George wished he were at home with the man there to help. He didn't want to wake up his friends. If he got a sponge from the sink maybe he could clean up the spill. But as he hurried across the kitchen, he slipped on the wet floor.

Poor George. Now he was homesick *and* wet. He started to sniffle.

The light in the kitchen went on. Gramma Willa scooped George and Lola up. She gave them a hug and dried them off. Then Gramma called the man with the yellow hat so George could hear his voice.

Tallulah and Jarrod woke up too and helped cheer George up.

"I was nervous about spending a night away from home at my first sleepover too," Tallulah confessed.

"Not me," Jarrod said proudly.

"That's because you haven't gone to one yet," Tallulah said.

"Have too. This one!" insisted Jarrod. Tallulah and George just smiled.

George felt better. He snuggled down into the sleeping
bag that Gramma spread on the living room couch. The
kids pulled their sleeping bags out of the tent and spread
them on the floor near George. Gramma left a small light
on over the desk. They all fell right to sleep.

And in the morning, George helped make
banana and chocolate chip waffles for breakfast.

When the man came to pick George up, he heard all about how fun the sleepover had been. George and the man thanked their friends and waved goodbye.

"So, George. Do you think you'll be ready for another sleepover sometime?" the man asked.

George was already packing for it!

THE END.

What DO Llamas Do?

written by Katy Torney
& illustrated by Leanne Pizio

L ike all the llamas on Katy's farm, Inca looked like the letter "L". She was named for her dignified Peruvian ancestors. Inca wasn't exactly dignified.

But she did know
how to have fun.

Llamaste and Dolly Llama looked dignified when they kushed like lazy cats near the baby crias. (Kushing is what llamas do when they fold their legs under them to rest.)

But that's not what Inca did.
She **POPPED** out of the barn
and scared Obama Llama.

That made Llamadeus sing out his warning cry.
All the llamas scurried toward him. But what did Inca
do? She spronged the other way.

(All llamas sprong, jumping straight up into the air.)

But Inca spronged so high she disturbed the llama mamas trying to calm their baby crias. And she spronged so fast that the boy llamas couldn't catch the girl llamas who followed her.

"Inca, you have to do what llamas do.
And don't sprong near those sleeping crias,"
Dolly llama hummed.

(Humming is what llamas do when they talk to each other.)

Inca had no time for Dolly's humming
when she heard Katy's llama-mobile.
She hurried to the gate, hoping that
maybe Katy would take her to school.
Inca wanted to help teach children
about the letter

Katy usually took Dolly Llama and every time they returned from school, Dolly boasted about how the children petted her, gave her treats and snuggly hugs. That sounded like fun to Inca.

But Dolly spat at her . . .

You're not
the kind of llama
children like!

You don't do
what llamas do!

On Valentine's Day, Inca heard the llama-mobile and galloped to the fence. Katy burst from the van with a fluffy pink hat. "Inca, do you want to wear a hat?" she asked. "Let's see if you're ready to teach the letter 'L'." Inca hopped into the llama-mobile.

WITH A START, the llama mobile moved ...

and MOVED ... and REALLY MOVED ...

Trees and buildings flew by. Tall things, small things, flashy-dashy things blurred together. Inca swayed to Katy's saucy singing ...

In school Inca waited **quietly** as the children surrounded her. She stood patiently while Katy told them how llamas give fleece for scarves, carry the marshmallows on camping trips and are the best friends you could ever have.

After the children's sticky pats and snuggly hugs, Katy declared, "Inca, you know just what llamas should do in a classroom!"

INCA
TEACHES THE
LETTER "L"

So Katy took Inca to teach the letter "L" . . .

in March . . . April . . . and May.

They taught the letter "L" during summer school . . .
in June . . . July . . . and August, too.

In August, the children watched
as Katy clipped Inca's fleece.
Then she cleaned and untangled
it, and spun it into yarn.

The children stared as Katy knitted Inca's fleece into a fluffy scarf.

No one was paying any attention to Inca . . .

... when she did something
llamas should **NEVER** do in a classroom.

She pooped!

"Inca, you know I love you," Katy said as she removed the bikini, "but that's not what llamas do in school." She sighed. "Maybe Dolly should teach the letter 'L' for a while."

Inca hung her head and slipped behind the barn.

So, in September, Dolly pranced to the llama-mobile in a sunflower hat.

She wore a witch's hat in October and a Pilgrim's hat in November.

Each time, before
they left, Katy
looked sad and gave
Inca a big hug.

On a December day, so cold that water froze in
the trough, Katy brought the most spectacular hat
Inca had ever seen. Katy placed it on Dolly's head,
but Dolly flung it off. She thought the blinking
lights didn't go with her hair.

The dazzling hat landed next to Inca who lowered her head and scooped it up. Soon Katy and Inca were sauntering into a classroom.

Inca stood quietly
while the children
learned, petted
and hugged her.

"You did just what llamas should do!" Katy said afterwards as they stood beside the llama-mobile and she gave Inca a big kiss.

Suddenly a fierce monster appeared in the window.

Its antlers glinted as if they were **ON FIRE**.

The monster looked ready to LEAP, and POUNCE, and EAT her . . .

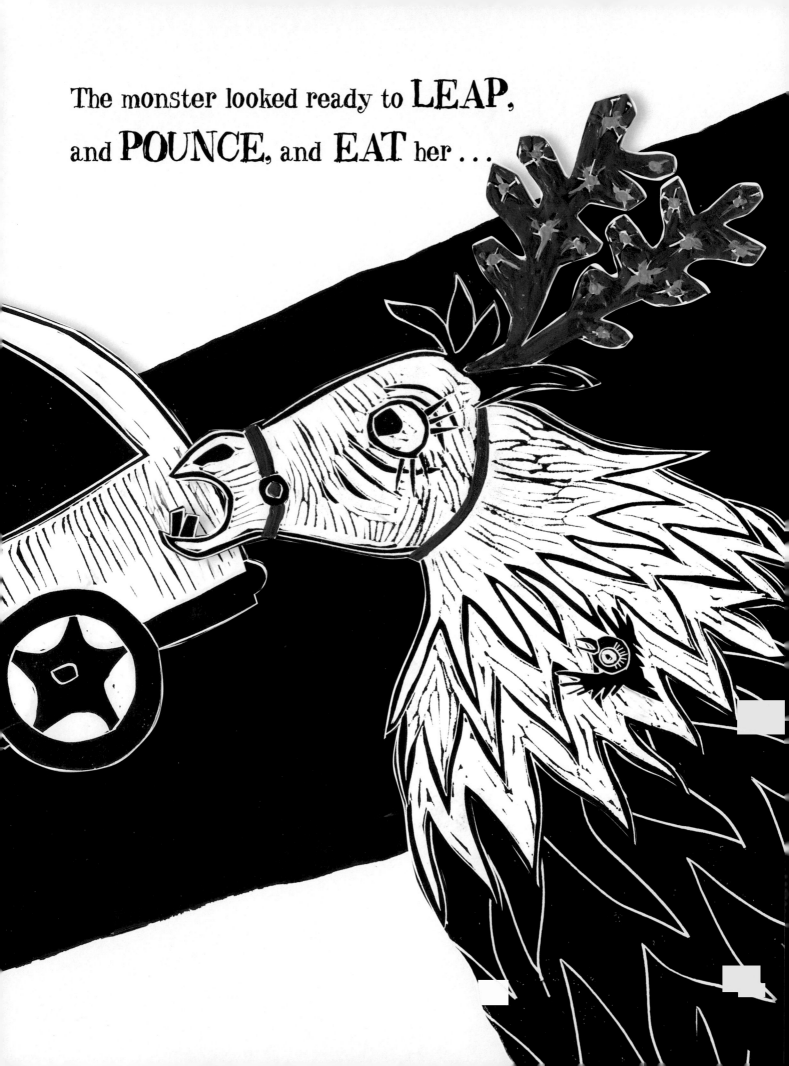

Inca bolted. "Inca," Katy called,
"It's only your reflection!"
But Inca . . .

. . . dashed across the parking lot . . .

. . . sped in front of the swing set . . .

outran a bicyclist, and raced . . .

galloped by the slide . . .

jumped over the see saw . . .

STOP

into the middle of a street . . .

... a very busy street, with cars moving even faster than a frightened llama.

Inca was far from her pasture, fence and barn. She was miles from Llamadeus' warnings and from Dolly who knew just what llamas do.

WHAT SHOULD SHE DO?

Then she remembered her name and Inca stood dignified like her ancestors. She waited patiently just as she did when the children hugged her.

Soon Katy was by her side. She gave the frightened llama a tight hug. "Inca," Katy said, "you have a special place in my heart. There isn't a llama anywhere who can do things the way *you* do!"

And as she hugged her, Katy was sure
she saw the flicker of a smile on Inca's lips.

What Do Llamas Do?

is based on a true story and Inca is real. Just as in the story, she doesn't always like to listen to her humans, and was a bit of a troublemaker when I took her to visit classrooms so we could teach the letter "L".

Llamas are very patient. That makes it easy for me to place hats on their heads. Usually they don't mind a bit. But that changed one cold December day in 2013 when Inca wore flashing antlers to celebrate the holiday season. As we left a classroom to head home, Inca spotted her reflection in the llama-mobile window and it scared her into bolting. Unfortunately, the school was only a slight distance from Friendly Avenue, one of the biggest roadways in Greensboro, North Carolina where we live. It took two police officers to recapture her while three police cars blocked six lanes of traffic for miles. Her escapade made the evening news.

Justin Douglas, one of the officers who caught her, is pictured here holding Inca's lead.

I dedicate this book
to the young children who found fun in learning the letter "L" with llamas, to the llamas who inspired them (especially Patches, the greatest llama of all), and to my children, Caitlin, Garret and Evin, who share the most special place in my heart.

My thanks also
to the dedicated and high-spronging efforts of Terry Atkinson, Steve Godwin, Leanne Pizio, and Susie Wilde.

PHOTO CREDIT: EVIN TORNEY PHOTOGRAPHY

Katy & Inca

Published by Catherine Torney, Greensboro, NC.
ISBN 978-0-692-92503-4